ISABEL
AND THE
HUNGRY COYOTE

Written by Keith Polette

Illustrated by Esther Szegedy

To my family.
⚊⚊ Keith

To Alain, who's always there.
⚊⚊ Esther

Text © 2009 by Keith Polette
Illustration © 2009 by Esther Szegedy

Polette, Keith.

    Isabel and the Hungry Coyote / written by Keith Polette; illustrated by Esther Szegedy;
–1st ed. –McHenry, IL: Raven Tree Press, 2009.

    p. ; cm.

    Summary: A retelling of the classic tale, Little Red Riding Hood.

English-Only Edition
ISBN: 978-1-934960-72-1 hardcover

Bilingual Edition
ISBN: 978-0-9724973-0-5 hardcover
ISBN: 978-0-9770906-4-8 paperback

    Audience: K–3 grade
    English-only or bilingual text with mostly English story and concept words in Spanish formats

    1. Self-reliance–Juvenile fiction. 2. Coyote–Juvenile fiction.
    3. Fairy tales. I. Illus. Szegedy, Esther. II. Title.

LCCN: 2009923418

Printed in Taiwan

10 9 8 7 6 5 4 3 2 1

First Edition

Free activities for this book are available at www.raventreepress.com

ISABEL
AND THE
HUNGRY COYOTE

Written by Keith Polette
Illustrated by Esther Szegedy

Raven Tree Press
A Division of Delta Systems Co., Inc.
www.raventreepress.com

Coyote's stomach rumbled as he prowled the desert looking for something to eat.

He suddenly stopped at the entrance to a small, dry valley. His yellow eyes flashed as he spotted a girl wearing a red hood. She was singing softly and picking desert flowers.

Licking his lips, Coyote silently crept towards the girl in red.

With his eyes narrowed into slits, Coyote inched closer and closer. The girl kept picking flowers.

When Coyote was just a few feet away, he got ready to pounce. But suddenly, his stomach rumbled. It churned and gurgled and grumbled!

The girl whirled around. "Mister Coyote!" she exclaimed. "What do you want?"

"Oh," said Coyote, as his stomach growled again. "I just wanted to say . . . ah . . . good morning."

"Well, good morning to you," said the girl taking a step back. "My name is Isabel."

"That is a pretty red hood you are wearing, Isabel," said Coyote.

His glowing eyes flared as he inched closer to her.

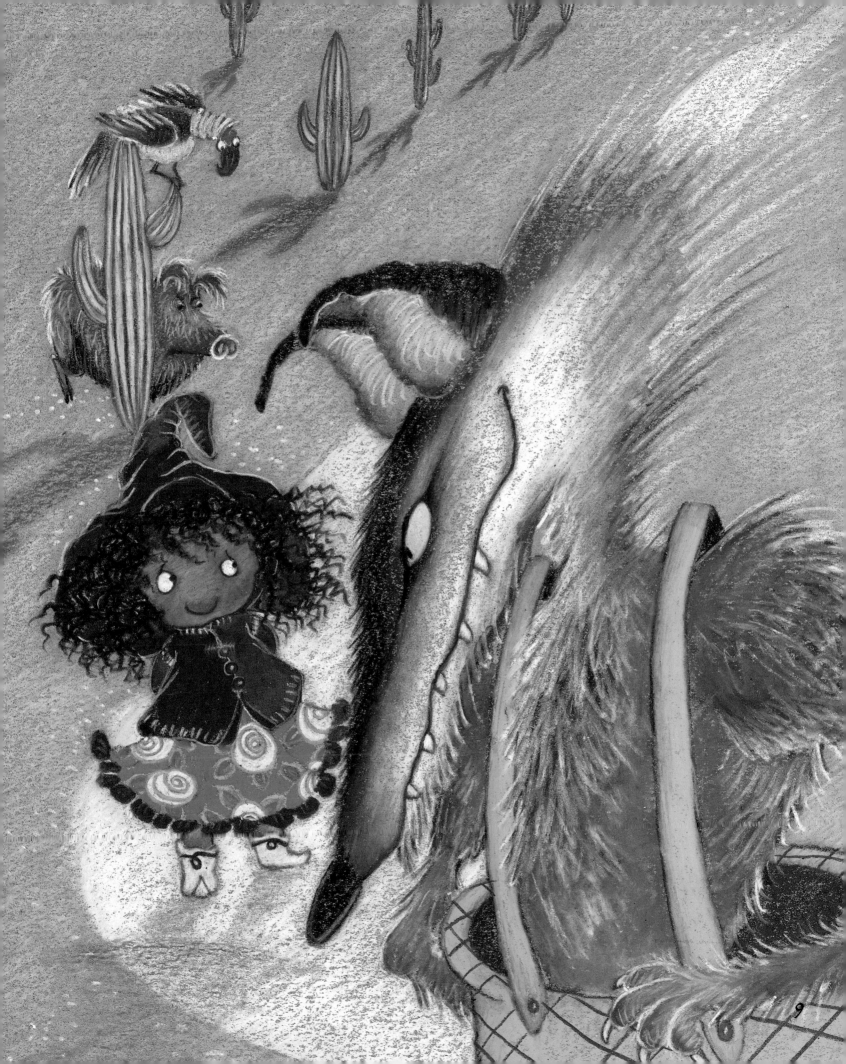

9

"Thank you, sir. This hood keeps the sun from my face," Isabel said as she took another step back.

"I see," said Coyote. "Where are you going?"

Coyote stepped even closer to her.

"I am going to visit my grandmother," said Isabel as she backed away from him.

"Is that so? And where does your grandmother live?" he asked slyly.

"She lives at the end of the valley," replied Isabel.

She pointed down the road. "Look, there is her house."

Coyote looked at the adobe house and then at Isabel. "This girl would make a fine lunch," he thought. "But if I wait, I can gobble up the girl and her grandmother," he schemed.

Coyote sniffed the air. "What do you have in the basket?"

"Spicy tamales and red chile sauce," said Isabel. "Would you like one?"

"Oh, no!" he said. "I never eat tamales and chile sauce. They taste like fire and burn my mouth!" snapped Coyote.

Coyote looked toward the house and said, "I have to go now. Goodbye."

"Goodbye," replied Isabel, her voice quivering.

Coyote kicked up a little dust as he scampered away. His yellow eyes flashed as he vanished in the direction of the grandmother's house.

When Coyote arrived at the house, he found the door wide open. Licking his lips, he snuck inside.

Coyote looked in each room, but he did not see Isabel's grandmother.

Just then, he heard Isabel lift the latch on the gate outside. Coyote hurried into the tidy bedroom and put on the grandmother's nightgown. He jumped into her bed and pulled the covers up to his chin.

When Isabel arrived, she called out, "Hello, Grandmother. Are you home?"

In a sweet voice, Coyote answered, "Yes, Isabel. Come in."

Isabel went straight to her grandmother's bedroom. Coyote said, "I am happy to see you, my dear. Come closer."

Isabel approached the bed. Then she stopped. "Grandmother, why do you have such big eyes?"

"My eyes are big so I can see you, my dear," said Coyote.

Isabel looked closely. "Grandmother, why do you have such big ears?"

"My ears are big so I can hear you, my dear," said Coyote.

Then Isabel gasped. "Grandmother, why do you have such big arms?"

"My arms are big so I can hug you, my dear," said Coyote.

Isabel cried out, "Grandmother, what a big, big mouth you have!"

"Little Isabel, I have big mouth . . . so I can eat you!" snarled Coyote.

With a terrible growl, Coyote leaped from the bed. He grabbed Isabel with his powerful arms and opened his big jaws to swallow her.

Isabel trembled as she looked into Coyote's wide mouth. She squirmed and tried to get away, but Coyote's arms were very strong!

Coyote opened his jaws even wider. Isabel stared into his cave-like mouth and suddenly got an idea. She threw the entire basket of tamales and chile sauce into Coyote's big trap.

Coyote bit down. Then he howled, "AIIIEEE! Tamales and chile sauce! My mouth is on fire!"

Coyote dropped Isabel and raced out of the house. He hurried through the gate and dashed into the valley, howling the entire time.

Isabel listened to his cries fade away into the desert.

Just then, the back door of the house opened. A voice said, "Hello, Isabel. I'm so happy to see you, my dear!"

Isabel turned and cried, "Oh, Grandmother!" The girl ran to hug her.

Isabel's grandmother said: "I was taking a nap in the backyard when a terrible howl woke me up."

Isabel nodded. "That was Coyote. He wanted to eat me for lunch, but I threw a basket of tamales and chile sauce into his big mouth!"

"You are a brave and clever girl!" Isabel's grandmother said with a smile.

"But Grandmother," said Isabel, "I brought those tamales and chile sauce for you."

"Don't worry, my dear," said her grandmother. "We can make some more."

And that is exactly what they did.